SWAMP WATER

BY
ROBERT MUNSCH

ILLUSTRATED BY
MICHAEL MARTCHENKO

Scholastic Canada Ltd.
New York Toronto London Auckland Sydney
Mexico City New Delhi Hong Kong Buenos Aires

Scholastic Canada Ltd.
604 King Street West, Toronto, Ontario M5V 1E1, Canada

Scholastic Inc.
557 Broadway, New York, NY 10012, USA

Scholastic Australia Pty Limited
PO Box 579, Gosford, NSW 2250, Australia

Scholastic New Zealand Limited
Private Bag 94407, Botany, Manukau 2163, New Zealand

Scholastic Children's Books
Euston House, 24 Eversholt Street, London NW1 1DB, UK

www.scholastic.ca

The illustrations in this book were painted in watercolour
on Crescent illustration board.
The type is set in 16 point ITC Leawood.

Library and Archives Canada Cataloguing in Publication

Munsch, Robert N., 1945-, author
Swamp water / by Robert Munsch ; illustrated by Michael
Martchenko.

ISBN 978-1-4431-2837-7 (pbk.)

I. Martchenko, Michael, illustrator II. Title.

PS8576.U575S93 2013a   jC813'.54   C2013-902742-4

6 5 4 3 2   Printed in Singapore 46   14 15 16 17 18

For Victoria Campbell,
Fredericton, New Brunswick
— R.M.

"Victoria," said her grandmother, "as my birthday present, I am going to take you out for a special lunch."

"Okay," said Victoria. "Let's go!"

So they walked and walked and walked and they came to a hamburger restaurant.

"HAMBURGERS!" said Victoria. "I love hamburgers. Especially with cheese and pickles and ketchup and mustard and whatever else they have to put on it."

"Please?

"Please?

"Please?

"PLEEEEEEEEASE?"

"No," said Grandma. "We go to hamburger restaurants all the time. It's not special."

So they walked and walked and walked and they came to a chicken restaurant.

"CHICKEN!" said Victoria. "I love chicken. Chicken fingers and french fries!"

"Please?

"Please?

"Please?

"Please?

"Please?

"PLEEEEEEEEASE?"

"No," said Grandma. "We go to chicken restaurants all the time. It's not special."

So they walked and walked and walked and they came to a taco restaurant.

"TACOS!" said Victoria. "I love tacos. Especially with cheese and onions and lettuce and tomatoes and whatever else they have to put on it."

"Please?

"Please?

"Please?

"Please?

"Please?

"Please?

"Please?

"PLEEEEEEEEASE?"

"No," said Grandma. "We go to taco restaurants all the time. It's not special."

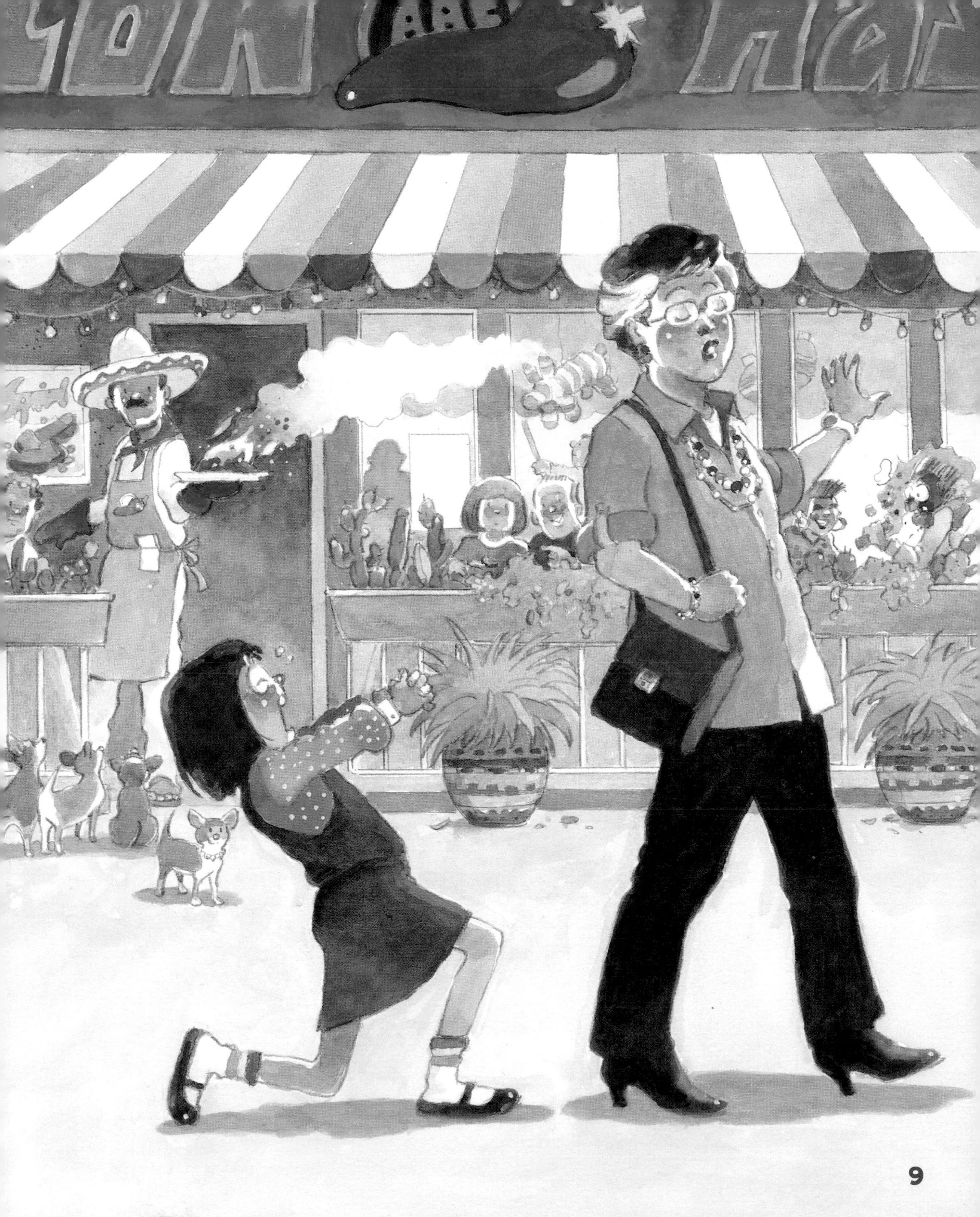

So they walked and walked and walked till they came to a very fancy restaurant.

"What is this place?" said Victoria. "I've never heard of it. They don't even advertise on TV. Are you sure I am going to like it?"

"Go inside and look out the back window," said Grandma.

"Wow!" said Victoria. "Ducks! Ducks in the river! This restaurant has ducks! I have never been to a restaurant with ducks before. Even hamburger restaurants do not have ducks!"

"It is a wonderful restaurant!" said Grandma. "I have been coming here since before you were born."

"A duck restaurant! This is really neat!" said Victoria.

Then a waiter came and said, "Would you like our Fancy Restaurant Fancy Lunch?"

"Yes," said Grandma.

"No," said Victoria.

"No?" said the waiter. "Well, what would you like?"

"I would like a hamburger," said Victoria.

"Ahhh," said the waiter. "We do not have hamburgers."

"Okay," said Victoria. "I would like chicken fingers and french fries."

"Ahhh," said the waiter. "We do not have chicken fingers and french fries."

"Then," said Victoria, "I would like tacos."

"Ahhh," said the waiter. "We do not have tacos."

Victoria thought for a minute and said, "I would like a peanut butter and jelly sandwich."

"Ahhh," said the waiter. "We do not have peanut butter and jelly sandwiches."

"No peanut butter and jelly sandwiches?" said Victoria.

"No," said the waiter. "Definitely not!"

"Well," said Victoria, "Do you have bread?"

"Yes," said the waiter.

"Do you have jelly?"

"Yes," said the waiter.

"Do you have peanut butter?"

"Yes," said the waiter.

"Then stick them together!" said Victoria. "It's called a peanut butter and jelly sandwich."

"NNNNNNO!" said the waiter.

Victoria ran into the kitchen and found the cook. "I am here for a special lunch," she said. "Can you please make me a peanut butter and jelly sandwich?"

"Peanut butter and jelly sandwiches are not on our fancy menu," said the cook.

Victoria said, "Do you have bread?"

"Yes," said the cook.

"Do you have jelly?"

"Yes," said the cook.

"Do you have peanut butter?"

"Yes," said the cook.

"Well, stick them together," said Victoria. "It's called a peanut butter and jelly sandwich."

"Okay!" said the cook. "I will make you a peanut butter and jelly sandwich."

"Good!" said Victoria. "And please cut it into little pieces. It has to be cut into very little pieces with no crust."

"Okay!" said the cook.

Victoria went back to the table.

The waiter came again and said, "And what would you like to drink?"

"Tea," said Grandma. "I love tea."

"How about our Famous English Breakfast Tea?" said the waiter.

"Lovely," said Grandma.

"And I," said Victoria, "would like swamp water."

"Swamp water?" yelled the waiter. "What is SWAMP WATER?"

"It is very easy to make," said Victoria. "Just mix cola and ginger ale and root beer and orange soda and chocolate milk till it is the colour of a swamp, and that is swamp water."

"NNNNNNNNNNNNO!" yelled the waiter.

"I want to see the cook," said Victoria.

"Oh, all right!" said the waiter. "We will make you swamp water."

So Victoria looked at the ducks and after a while the waiter brought her swamp water and a peanut butter and jelly sandwich that was cut into little pieces. Even the crust was cut off.

"WOW!" said Victoria. "This is perfect. Thank you very much."

"You're welcome," said the waiter.

Then Victoria opened the window and threw her sandwich to the ducks.

"AHHHHHHHHHHHHHHHHHHHHHHHH!!!!" yelled the waiter. "You can't feed your lunch to the ducks!"

"I just did feed my lunch to the ducks," said Victoria.

"Thank you, Grandma!" said Victoria. "This is a wonderful restaurant."

"Yes," said Grandma. "Yes, it is a wonderful restaurant. It is a wonderful DUCK restaurant, and this is a special lunch, and I am having a wonderful time."

Then Grandma called the waiter and said, "My granddaughter would like ten more fancy restaurant peanut butter sandwiches please, and take off the crust. I do not think that the ducks like crust."

And ten more peanut butter
sandwiches is what they got.